EVIL EYES

Carlo Armenise

Author's Tranquility Press
ATLANTA, GEORGIA

Copyright © 2024 by Carlo Armenise

All rights reserved. No part of this publication may be reproduced, distributed or transmitted in any form or by any means, including photocopying, recording, or other electronic or mechanical methods, without the prior written permission of the publisher, except in the case of brief quotations embodied in critical reviews and certain other noncommercial uses permitted by copyright law. For permission requests, write to the publisher, addressed "Attention: Permissions Coordinator," at the address below.

Carlo Armenise / Author's Tranquility Press
3900 N Commerce Dr. Suite 300 #1255
Atlanta, GA 30344, USA
www.authorstranquilitypress.com

Ordering Information:
Quantity sales. Special discounts are available on quantity purchases by corporations, associations, and others. For details, contact the "Special Sales Department" at the address above.

Evil Eyes / Carlo Armenise
Paperback: 978-1-964037-38-7
eBook: 978-1-964037-42-4

Contents

Chapter One 1

Chapter Two 24

Chapter Three 40

Chapter Four 57

Chapter Five 69

Chapter One

It's said beauty is in the eye of the beholder. However, since the definition of beauty can differ from beholder to beholder, it means beauty changes from eye to eye. Forty-year-old Andrew Wyler understood true beauty better than most. As a world-famous fashion photographer, capturing images of beautiful women has been his passion for over twenty years. But while he was always around women, he hadn't found that special one that captured his heart and made him want to settle down. Until he met Elizabeth. Elizabeth Simon was a thirty-five-year-old model of Swedish descent. She had piercing blue eyes and long, flowing blonde hair. She wasn't only beautiful; she had a simple elegance and a sweet disposition. Despite being one of the world's top models, she had an enduring modesty that attracted Andrew. They met on a modeling shoot, and a 'love at first sight' romance led to an engagement party six months later at the house of his best friend, forty-year-old Terry Washington. Terry was the top black modeling agent in the country. He and Andrew met at the beginning of their careers and developed an honest, deep respect for one another's talents. Terry for finding beauty, and Andrew for showing it to the world. Terry's house was a several-leveled, elaborate, castle-like mansion that he had built as a shrine to his narcissistic ego.

The engagement party was already going on when Andrew and Elizabeth arrived. The party guest list included the world's top models, all the principles from every modeling agency, and at least a hundred members of the fashion industry press. While everyone was dancing to the sounds of a live band and having a good time, Andrew and Terry were sitting at an outside bar having a drink.

"You sure you want to do this?" Terry asked.

"You mean have a drink?" Andrew replied jokingly.

"That's funny, but this decision is no laughing matter. You're committing your life to another person."

"I know, but I'm ready to commit. All the beautiful women I've been with haven't made me happy. It's not just about sex; it's about finding that special woman to share my life and grow old with."

"I've got all the 'special women' I can handle without getting married, and I think you're crazy to give up your freedom."

"Isn't it about time you settle down yourself?"

"Settle down? Are you crazy? I have to increase my debauchery to make up for you," Terry said, laughing and holding up his glass. "Cheers. I wish you and Liz all the best."

"Thank you," Andrew said, touching his glass with Terry's and drinking. "And thank you for throwing us this party."

"It's my pleasure. Now come with me," Terry said, leading Andrew back into the house to the bandstand.

"Can I have your attention, please," Terry yelled as he and Andrew climbed onto the bandstand, and Terry grabbed a microphone. "Come on, you moochers, stop partying for a minute and gather around the bandstand. I'm going to make a toast. Would Elizabeth Simon please join us?"

As the crowd gathered around the bandstand, servers poured champagne for the toast, and Elizabeth walked out of a nearby bathroom. "There she is, in the bathroom, already contemplating suicide," Terry joked.

The crowd laughed, and Elizabeth joined Terry and Andrew on the bandstand, kissed Andrew, and the crowd applauded.

"You can tell they're not married yet," Terry joked. "But seriously, the reason we're all here tonight, besides drinking my booze, is to celebrate the engagement of this beautiful, unsuspecting young woman to this not-so-good-looking, questionable old man."

The crowd laughed and applauded.

"And as the best man to my best friend, I want to propose a toast," he said, and everyone raised their champagne glasses. "To Liz and Andy, may you have a life filled with health, love, money, and fun. And I hope some of that also carries over into your married life. Cheers."

Everyone takes a drink, and Andrew steps up to the microphone.

"Thank you all for coming and sharing this special occasion with me."

"With us," Elizabeth says into the mic.

"Right," Andrew says, pulling her close. "With us. And we want to thank Terry for throwing us this wonderful party," he says, holding his glass up to Terry, and the crowd applauds. "And I want you all to know that I'm the luckiest man in the world," he says, kissing Liz.

"What can I say? When he's right, he's right," Liz says, and the crowd laughs and applauds.

"Okay, let's all get back to partying," Terry says, and the band starts to play. "Come on, Liz," he says, taking her hand. "Dance with a good dancer for a change."

"No, I'll take my chances with you," she says, kissing Andrew and dancing with Terry.

Andrew walks to a bar near the dance floor and sits on a bar stool.

"Scotch and water, please," he says to the bartender.

The bartender hands him the drink, and while he watches Liz and Terry dance, a gorgeous thirty-year-old model sits beside him at the bar.

"Black Russian, please," she says to the bartender.

The bartender makes the drink and hands it to her.

"Thank you," she says and turns to Andrew.

"Congratulations on your engagement, Mr. Wyler."

Andrew turns to the woman and is immediately captivated by her beauty. Her facial features are perfect, like a DaVinci painting, but her most attractive feature is her big, hypnotic, and mesmerizing black eyes. Andrew is so enamored that he stares at her momentarily before he speaks.

"I'm sorry. Do I know you?"

"Not technically, but any respectable model has heard of the great Andrew Wyler, the world's greatest photographer."

"I don't know about the world, this room maybe," he says, smiling.

"A modest man, how refreshing," she replies. "You don't usually find too much modesty in this business," she says and extends her hand to shake. "My name is Isabella Rossini."

"That's a pretty name," Andrew replies, shaking her hand. "Very Italian."

"I was named after my Italian grandmother on my mother's side."

"She must be beautiful."

"She was, but I'm prettier," she replies jokingly.

Andrew smiles. "And you're a model."

"Well, sort of. I just started a few months ago, so I haven't worked much yet, but I hope to. Got any tips for a new model from a famous photographer's point of view?"

"That's an interesting question. Let's see, I know, be careful not to fall into the model syndrome."

"Model syndrome? Isabella asks.

"That's when a model gets too enamored with her beauty and forgets that physical beauty is only skin deep and doesn't make up for a bad attitude. Trust me, in this business, there are a lot of cutthroat egos willing to take advantage of you for their benefit."

"I know. I've already come across a few. What about you? You don't have an ego."

"Sure, I do, but I try to keep it in check and remember what goes around comes around," he says and smiles.

The dance finishes, and Liz stays on the dance floor talking to another model as Terry walks over to the bar.

"I see you've met my newest acquisition," Terry tells Andrew, indicating Isabella.

"Yes, but she didn't tell me she was with your agency."

"Just signed her last week."

"I was told he was the best," Isabella says.

"I've always been attracted to intelligent women," Terry says, smiling, and they laugh as Elizabeth walks up.

"Come on, sweetheart," Elizabeth says to Andrew. "Let's dance, the tops of my feet need a break," she says, smiling at Terry.

"Funny, my feet feel fine," Terry replies, laughing.

"Liz, I want you to meet Isabella Rossini," Andrew says. "She's a new model with Terry's agency. Isabella, this is my fiancé' Elizabeth Simon."

"I know who you are," Isabella says, shaking Liz's hand. "You're the reason I got into modeling. You're so beautiful."

"Thank you," Liz replies.

"I hope we'll have the opportunity to work together," Isabella says.

"Don't worry. I'm sure Terry will make that happen."

"Absolutely," Terry says.

"Now, if you'll excuse us, I want to dance with my future husband," Liz says, pulling Andrew up from his barstool.

"It was nice meeting you," Andrew says to Isabella.

"Likewise," Isabella replies, giving him a seductive smile. "And thanks for the tip."

While Isabella watches, Andrew and Liz walk onto the dance floor and start to dance.

"Do you know her?" Liz asks Andrew.

"Who?"

"That model, Isabella."

"No, we just met tonight. Why?"

"Because I think she's after more than just pictures from you."

"Don't be ridiculous. She's just starting in the business and wanted some pointers."

"That better be all she wants."

"Is that jealousy I hear?" Andrew says, smiling.

"No, it's PMS, and homicide isn't out of the question," she replies jokingly.

"You've got nothing to worry about. I love you, and you're the only woman I want," he replies, kissing her.

"And it better stay that way."

After the dance, Terry approaches Andrew.

"Ready for a game?" Terry asks.

"You still haven't paid me what you owe me from the last time we played," Andrew replies.

"So, we'll call it double or nothing. Let's go," Terry said.

"This won't take long," Andrew said to Liz, kissed her, and followed Terry into a nearby game room equipped with a hand-carved pool table.

"Since you won at eight ball the last time, I get to break," Terry said as he racked the balls.

"Go ahead, but it won't help."

"We'll see," Terry replies, shoots the break, and nothing goes in.

"I told you," Andrew says as he studies the table for his shot. "Tell me more about that new model, Isabella."

"Pretty, huh?"

"Gorgeous. Incredible eyes. Where did you find her?"

"I didn't, she found me. She walked into my office and said she had just returned from modeling in Europe and wanted to find an agent."

"She wasn't represented over there?"

"No, said she was representing herself."

"Strange. With her look, you think we would have heard of her."

"Yeah, but I'm not complaining. Less drama. Now, unless you're trying to bore me into submission, shoot the fucking ball."

"Seven ball in the side pocket," Andrew says and shoots the shot.

As the shot goes in, hand clapping is heard, and Terry and Andrew look toward the game room door and see Isabella.

"Nice shot," she says, walking over to the table and standing beside Andrew.

"Thank you," Andrew replies.

"I'm getting sober; I need a drink," Terry says and hands his cue stick to Isabella. "You fill in for me."

"You better come back. You owe me money." Andrew says as Terry leaves the room.

"You two are like my brothers, always betting, "she smiles.

"Do you play?" Andrew asks.

"Not very well. I don't even remember how to hold the cue stick," she says, fumbling with the stick.

"Would you like me to show you?"

"Please."

Andrew stands behind her, puts his arms around her waist, and grips his hands over hers on the cue stick.

"That's it," Andrew says.

She sets the cue on the table, turns around, and gives Andrew an intense, seductive stare, and he falls into a trance. Unaware of what he's doing, he pulls her close and is about to kiss her when Elizabeth walks into the room and sees them.

"You asshole," Liz screams at Andrew and runs out of the room.

Elizabeth's voice broke the trance, and Andrew dropped the cue stick on the table and ran after her.

"Liz, wait."

With a look of satisfaction, Isabella smiles, picks up the cue stick, and makes a shot.

Elizabeth, crying, walks out of the house next to a pool and sits in a deck chair as Andrew walks out and approaches her.

"Liz, what's the matter?" He asks, attempting to put his arm around her.

"Get away from me," she says and pushes him away.

"What are you so upset about?"

"You were just about to kiss Isabella."

"What? I was showing her how to hold the cue stick."

"Don't give me that bullshit; I saw you."

"That's ridiculous."

"Are you calling me a liar? I know what I saw."

"Look, baby, I don't know what you think you saw, but you're overreacting."

"I told you that model wanted you."

"You have to believe me. I only want you, and there will never be anyone else. I want to marry you and spend the rest of my life with you," he hugs her.

"Are you sure? Because if not, we can call off the wedding."

"I've never been surer of anything in my life."

Liz pauses and hugs him. "Maybe I did overreact."

"You did," he says and kisses her. "Come on, let's go back to the party."

"You go ahead. I need a minute to pull myself together."

"Don't take too long. I want to dance. I love you," he says.

"I love you, too," she replies and kisses him.

Andrew walks back into the house and passes Isabella at the pool door.

"Is she okay?" she asks.

"She's fine. Just stressed about the wedding. Excuse me," he says and walks into the house.

After Andrew leaves, Isabella walks out to Elizabeth.

"Are you okay?"

"Don't patronize me, you bitch," Liz says angrily. "You're not fooling me; I know what you're up to."

"What's the matter? Afraid he'd rather be with me?" Isabella says, smiling.

"You're fucking crazy," Liz replies. "As long as I'm in his life, he'll never be with you."

Evil Eyes

"You're right, so I'll have to do something about that," Isabella says, locking eyes with Liz and giving her an evil stare.

At that moment, a giant dragonfly appears out of nowhere and attacks Liz's head. She swings at the fly, trying to knock it away, while Isabella watches Liz swing at nothing but air. The fly is an illusion manifested by Isabella. As Liz swings at the fly, it flies into her mouth and down her throat. Chocking, Liz falls over a deck chair, hits her head on the side of the pool, and falls into the water. Struggling to keep her head above water but still choking on the imaginary fly and unable to breathe, she disappears under the water and drowns. Isabella, smiling, walks over to the pool and sees Liz's lifeless body floating.

"I told you I'd do something," she says, smiling, then walks back to the door and screams into the house.

"Help, there's been an accident."

Hearing Isabella's scream, several partygoers, including Andrew and Terry, run out to the pool, see Liz's body, jump in, and drag her body out of the pool.

"Someone call 911," Terry yells while Andrew administers CPR.

"Come on, Liz, breathe. Please breathe," he says frantically as she dies. "No, Liz, you can't die; I love you and need you in my life," he says, hugging her lifeless body and crying.

"I'm so sorry," Terry says, trying to console Andrew.

Andrew doesn't respond and keeps hugging her.

Considering Andrew's prominence in the modeling world, Liz's funeral was celebrated. Hundreds of people, including Isabella, attended the church service and the graveyard and offered their condolences to Andrew.

"I'm so sorry for your loss," Isabella said to Andrew at the gravesite.

"Thank you."

"In a way, I feel responsible. If I had seen her in the pool sooner, she might still be alive."

"It wasn't your fault," Andrew replied. "If anyone's to blame, it's me. I shouldn't have left her out there alone. She was too upset."

"Terry's agency has my number if I can do anything."

"Thank you."

As Isabella leaves, Terry walks up.

"How are you holding up?"

"Shitty," Andrew replies. "I haven't been able to sleep since it happened. I keep seeing her lying dead on the side of the pool."

"You've had a rough couple of years. First, you lose your parents and then Liz. You need to get away to rest and grieve."

"I thought about it, but I can't be alone. I need to work and be around people. Got any shoots coming up?"

Evil Eyes

"Trutardi's new perfume shoot is scheduled in two weeks," Terry replies.

"I'll do it."

"Are you sure?"

"Yes. I need to, for my sanity."

"Okay, whatever you say. I'll set it up. Let's get a drink."

"No, thanks. I'm going to hang out here for a little while."

"I'll call you with the details of the shoot," Terry says and walks away.

"Hey," Andrew says.

"Yeah?" Terry says, turning back to Andrew.

"Thanks for being there for me."

"You've been there for me a few times. I'll talk to you later."

As Terry walks away, Andrew picks up some flowers, walks over to Liz's gravesite, and watches as her coffin is lowered into her grave.

"I'll always love you, Liz. Rest in peace," he says, throwing the flowers on top of the coffin.

The Trutardi perfume photoshoot was held in a large warehouse. The crew, including Andrew, was busy setting up the photo equipment in front of a large, wooden volcano. The volcano had five platforms built into its sides and the top for models to stand on. At the back of each platform, gas jets were installed to create fire and give the volcano a simulated activity. Andrew makes the final adjustments to the camera as Bernie, the crew boss carrying a megaphone, walks up.

"All set for the test," Andy."

"Thanks, Bernie. Let's do it."

Bernie climbs up the volcano and stands on one of the side platforms.

"Fire 'em up," Bernie says in the megaphone, and flames appear behind each platform.

"How is it, Bernie?" Andrew says as he looks at the volcano through the camera lens.

Bernie looks back at the flames and sees them safely away from the front of the platform.

"Completely safe," Bernie says.

"Let's try the wind," Andrew says as he rechecks the camera.

"Blow it," Bernie says into the megaphone and two large fans in front of the volcano are turned on, and the flames flutter safely.

"Good to go, Bernie?"

"The flames aren't even close," Bernie says.

"Perfect," Andrew says, checking the shot in the camera. "We're ready. Cut the special effects and bring out the girls."

Evil Eyes

The flames and wind are turned off, and Bernie climbs off the volcano, walks over to three portable dressing rooms near the volcano, and knocks on the doors.

"Let's go, ladies; it's showtime."

A moment later, a young Spanish model named Maria, followed by Isabella and three other twenty-something models, walked out of the dressing rooms wearing skimpy African tribal costumes and followed Bernie to the volcano. Isabella and Andrew see one another.

"This is a surprise," Andrew says. "I didn't know you were on this shoot."

"Terry called me this morning and asked if I could fill in for someone who got sick. How are you?"

"I'm better. Thanks for asking."

Before Isabella can say anything else, Maria walks up, pushes her out of the way, and grabs Andrew's arm.

"If you're done talking to the extras, Andrew. The real talent is ready," she says, giving Isabella a disgusted look.

"We'll talk later," Andrew says to Isabella. "Okay, Bernie, let's get the girls in position on the volcano."

"Maria," Bernie says. "You'll be standing on the top platform holding a bottle of perfume, and the rest of you ladies will be standing on each side holding flowers. Got it? Okay, take your positions."

A prop girl hands Maria a perfume bottle and flowers to each of the other models, and they walk to the stairs leading up to the platforms. As Isabella starts to climb the stairs, Maria pushes her out of the way.

"The star of the shoot goes up first, sweety," Maria sneers and climbs the stairs.

Isabella and the other models follow Maria up the stairs and take positions on the side platforms holding the flowers while Maria stands on the top holding the perfume bottle.

"Hold up the perfume bottle, Maria. And look at it adoringly," Andrew says, looking into the camera.

Maria holds up the perfume bottle and poses as Andrew starts taking pictures.

"That's great. Now, the rest of you hold up your flowers and look up at the perfume bottle Maria's holding.

The models all hold up their flowers and look up at Maria.

"Perfect. Okay, Bernie, start the flames."

"Light them up," Bernie says, and the gas jets are turned on, and the flames appear behind each of the models.

"Looks good," Andrew says, looking into the camera. "Start the wind."

"Blow it," Bernie says.

Evil Eyes

The fans are turned on, and the flames safely flicker behind the models.

"It looks great," Andrew says, taking pictures.

Isabella looks up at Maria and gives her a menacing stare, and Maria suddenly imagines the flames catching her costume on fire. She drops the perfume bottle and starts to scream.

"Help, I'm on fire," she screamed, trying to put out the imaginary flames.

Andrew and the rest of the crew are watching but don't see anything.

"What's wrong with her?" Andrew asks Bernie. "She's not on fire."

"Got me," Bernie replies.

Continuing to scream for help, Maria, now imagining the flames are covering her whole body, tries to tear her costume off, falls off the volcano, and lands on the concrete warehouse floor. The crew, Andrew, and the rest of the models run over to her and find her unconscious. Andrew checks her pulse.

"She's still alive. Call 911," Andrew says to Bernie.

While Bernie makes the calls, Isabella approaches Andrew.

"Is she going to be all right?"

"I don't know," Andrew replies. "She thought she was on fire."

"I know. That's so strange," Isabella replies.

Later, as ambulance attendants put Maria in the ambulance and drove off, Terry walked into the warehouse.

"What happened?" he asks Andrew.

"Maria thought her costume caught fire and fell off the volcano trying to put it out."

"And she wasn't on fire?" Terry asks.

"No. She must have been hallucinating."

"What did the paramedics say?"

"They said she fractured her skull and broke her back. She may never walk again," Andrew replies.

"Man, that's terrible. I'll contact our insurance and ensure she's taken care of," Terry says.

"That's good because she's going to need a lot of care," Andrew replies.

"At the risk of sounding mercenary and insensitive," Terry says. "Did you finish the shoot before she fell?"

"No, we had just started."

"I know everybody's pretty shaken up, but you know Trutardi, if he doesn't have the shots by the end of the week, he'll sue me," Terry says.

"I understand," Andrew replies. "We could have one of the other models take her place on top of the volcano and finish."

"Good idea," Terry says and looks over at the models.

Isabella locks eyes with him and smiles.

"Let's have Isabella do it," Terry says. "She'll be perfect."

"I agree," Andrew replies.

Isabella replaces Maria and Andrew finishes the shoot. As the crew tears down the volcano and packs up the equipment, Andrew is packing his camera as Isabella, in street clothes, walks up.

"Need some help?"

"No, but thanks for asking. You were great today."

"Thank you, but I feel terrible getting the job at Maria's expense."

"Don't feel that way. You had nothing to do with her accident, and we had to finish the shoot today."

"Have you heard more about what caused her to act like that?" Isabella asks innocently.

"No, but it sounds like she must have been on drugs of some sort," Andrew replies as Terry walks up.

"You looked sensational in the shots, Isabella. I know the perfume company will be pleased," he says.

"Thank you, but the photographer deserves all the credit," she replies, smiling at Andrew.

"Trust me, he gets it," Terry says jokingly. "Listen, Andrew, I got a call from the Cosmo people, and they want me to put together a fashion shoot for next Friday. You interested?"

"I don't think so. I said I wanted to work, but after what happened today, I think I'll take your advice and rest for a while."

"Good idea. But call me if you want a golf lesson while you're resting."

"You mean a lesson in accurately counting strokes?" Andrew replies, laughing.

"I could have sworn those were all birdies," Terry replies. "Anyway, get some rest, and we'll talk. And Isabella, thanks again for standing in, and I promise you're going to work a lot," he says.

"That's great. Thank you."

Terry leaves, and Andrew finishes packing his camera equipment.

"I'll carry the tripod for you," she says, picking up the tripod.

"Thank you," Andrew says as he picks up the rest of the equipment, and they walk to his car.

"It's a good idea to get away and get some rest," Isabella says. "Got a favorite place to go when you need time for yourself?"

"Not really; I never take time for myself."

"Well, in that case, I might have the perfect spot for you. I'm renting a beautiful house at the beach. It's quiet, has spectacular views, and is perfect for resting."

"It sounds great, but I couldn't impose on you."

"You won't be imposing. I'm going to visit a girlfriend for a week, so the house will be sitting empty. What do you say?"

"Well, it sounds great. I'll do it."

"Fantastic. If you give me your number, I'll text you the address," Isabella says."

Andrew takes out a business card and hands it to Isabella.

"My home number is the top one," he says.

Isabella looks at the card.

"I'm happy I can help," Isabella says, smiling seductively.

"Me, too," Andrew replies.

Chapter Two

Andrew was looking forward to resting as he pulled up to the modern two-story house, his jeep packed with supplies. The house's location was even better than Isabella said. It was secluded and quiet, and the only sounds were waves hitting the nearby ocean shoreline.

"Isabella was right; this is a perfect place to rest," he says, unloading his jeep, finding the front door key under the front mat, and going in. He looks around and sets his luggage down in the living room. The interior of the house was spectacular. The design was a combination of modern and rustic with twenty-foot beamed ceilings, surrounded by floor-to-ceiling windows, that made the outside panorama seem like it was in the room. It was painted with soft pastel colors and filled with modern but comfortable furniture.

Andrew looks around the rest of the first floor and finds an office, an exercise room, a large bedroom, and an ultra-modern kitchen next to an outdoor patio and an Olympic-sized swimming pool. He walks onto the deck, looks at the spectacular hilltop view, takes a deep breath, inhales the fresh ocean air, and smiles. Then he went back inside and up to the upper level of the house

Evil Eyes

and found several closed doors on both sides of a long, pastel-painted hallway. He opens each door and finds a master suite and three guest bedroom suites, each with a balcony. Each bedroom was furnished with modern furniture, including a king-sized bed with nightstands, a dresser, a make-up table, a flat-screen T.V., and a large walk-in closet. On the walls were several professional modeling shots of Isabella in different outfits and poses. As Andrew looks at the photos, he's captivated by the power of her beautiful black eyes. He brings his luggage into one of the bedrooms, unpacks and walks out on the balcony. Lit by the sun's brilliance as it sets behind the hillside, Andrew looks out over the countryside and listens to the peaceful sounds of the ocean waves, then has dinner and gets ready for bed.

Andrew is lying in bed reading in his underwear. He sets the book down, turns off the light, and looks at the modeling shot of Isabella on the wall again. In the shot, Isabella is wearing a sexy black negligee and posing seductively on a bed. As he looks at her eyes in the photo, he falls asleep and dreams. In his dream, Isabella, wearing the same nightgown as in the picture, walks out of the bathroom in the bedroom and over to the bed, where Andrew, now naked, is waiting for her. She takes off the nightgown, revealing her gorgeous nude body, gets in bed next to Andrew, and they make love.

The following morning, an alarm from his phone wakes Andrew, with memories of the dream still in his head. He puts on his clothes and walks onto the balcony. Replaying the dream, he looks out over the countryside and sees a car approaching the house. He goes to the front door as the car pulls into the driveway and sees Isabella driving a sportscar with a large German Shepherd in the passenger seat.

"This is a pleasant surprise," Andrew says.

"I thought I'd stop by and make sure you're settled," she says, smiling.

"Oh yeah, everything is fantastic. The house, the ocean, the peace, it's all great. Thank you again for letting me stay here."

"You're very welcome."

"Who's the big guy sitting next to you?" Andrew asks.

"This is Night," she replies. "Say hello to Andrew, Night."

The dog barks calmly and looks at Andrew.

"Can I pet him?"

"Absolutely."

Andrew walks over to Night, pets him, and the dog licks his hand.

"He likes you," Isabella says to Andrew.

"He doesn't know me well enough," he replies, smiling.

"Sure, he does. He's very perceptive. He knows good people when he meets them – just like his mom," she says, giving Andrew a loving look. "Well, we've got to go and let you rest," she says, starting the car.

"Wait," Andrew says. "Before you go, can I ask you for a big favor?"

"Certainly. What is it?"

"I don't know how to operate your espresso machine, and I've got to have a cup of coffee. Would you and Night help me out?"

"What do you think, Night? Should we help him?"

Night jumps out of the car and runs into the house.

"I think that's a yes," Isabella says, turning off the car and following Andrew into the house.

Isabella makes the coffee, and then she and Andrew take their coffee onto the pool patio and sit while Night lays beside Isabella.

"Thank you for this," Andrew says, sipping his coffee.

"I'm the same way. Coffee comes first," Isabella replies. "Can I ask you a question?"

"Of course."

"Why did you become a photographer?"

"Because of my dad. He was a photographer and took me on shoots to help with his equipment. He was an artist with a camera, and watching him work made me decide to follow in his footsteps. And what about you? Why modeling? I mean, besides the obvious," he says, smiling.

"In my case, it was my mother. She pushed me to model and use my beauty to make money and support myself so I wouldn't have to rely on a man."

"And she was right," Andrew replies. "Are you and your mother close?"

"We were until she was killed in a car accident when I was fifteen years old."

"I'm so sorry," Andrew replied. "My parents were both killed in a car accident, too, two years ago."

Oh my God!" Isabella exclaims. "Do you know how the accident happened?"

"My parents were coming home from a party, and my dad was drunk and hit a tree. Their car blew up, and my parents were incinerated in the fire."

"How terrible," Isabella said and took his hand for comfort.

"How'd the accident happen that killed your mother?"

"She was pregnant, and we were on our way to the hospital to have my stepsister when she went into labor and lost control of the car."

"So, you were in the car with her?"

Isabella pauses as tears swell in her eyes, "Yes. I survived the crash, but my mother and stepsister died."

"Where was your father?"

"My mother and father divorced when I was ten, and when I was thirteen, my mother started seeing another man who got her pregnant, but he left her when he found out."

"What a slimeball," Andrew says and squeezes her hand.

"Yes. Anyway, I don't want to talk about sad things anymore. Let's talk about your photography. You're so talented."

"Thank you. But it's easy to take beautiful pictures when I'm taking pictures of women like you."

"Thank you," she says and gives him a seductive stare.

At that moment, he slips into the same trance Isabella put him in when they were playing pool, and he moves close and gives her a passionate kiss.

Later that afternoon, Isabella and Andrew are in bed naked, snuggling after making love. Andrew is lost in thought, staring at the ceiling and not talking.

"Was the sex that bad?" Isabella asked.

"What?" Andrew says, turning his attention to Isabella.

"You haven't said anything in almost an hour. So, I'm just wondering if you're disappointed?"

"No, it was wonderful. But I can't figure out what came over me."

"What do you mean," Isabella asked.

"I mean, I just lost Elizabeth, who I loved, and having sex with another woman this soon was the furthest thing from my mind."

"I understand. Should we stop seeing one another?"

"No, but I would like to take it a little slower and get to know one another."

"I'd like that," Isabella says and kisses him.

A few months later, Andrew and Terry get dressed after playing racquetball at the gym.

"You seemed a little distracted today," Terry says.

"What are you talking about? I beat you three out of four games," Andrew replies.

"That's my point. I won a game," Terry replies jokingly. "I was surprised you found time to play. Since you stopped working, you've spent all your time with Isabella. She must be a great piece of ass."

"Don't call my future wife a piece of ass," Andrew replies defensively.

"Future wife?"

"That's right. I'm going to ask her to marry me."

"But you just met her."

"I know it's quick, but I've never felt this way about anyone, including Liz, and we were together for two years."

"That's right, you and Liz were together for two years before you asked her to marry you."

"I know it sounds crazy,"

"It doesn't just sound crazy, it is crazy. Andrew, as your best friend, did you ever consider that your feelings for Isabella are just a rebound, and you're trying to replace your feelings for Liz?"

"No, my feelings for Isabella are real, and I'm not waiting."

"Sounds like you've made up your mind. And while I'm happy for you, don't say I didn't warn you."

"And you'll be my best man again?"

"Absolutely," Terry says and hugs Andrew.

A few weeks later, Andrew and Terry are dressed in tuxedos and sitting at a bar in an upscale hotel.

"Do you think we have a drinking problem?" Terry asks Andrew.

"Why?"

"Because we're always sitting at a bar drinking," Terry says, smiling.

"Well, after the wedding, I won't be going to bars anymore."

"I know; marriage does that," Terry replies. "I guess I'll have to find a new drinking buddy."

"Don't worry, being married isn't going to stop me from beating you once a week at racquetball," Andrew says, smiling.

"That's great. The only thing Isabella won't get in the way of is my weekly ass-kicking," he says sarcastically, laughing.

"Come on," Andrew says, checking his watch. "It's almost time; we need to get to the ballroom so I can get married."

The wedding ceremony was exquisite, and Isabella was ravishing in her beautiful white wedding gown. After the ceremony, the reception started, and Isabella, Andrew, and the other guests were dancing.

"Are you happy, Mrs. Wyler?" Andrew asks Isabella.

"So happy," she replies and kisses him. "This is a dream come true."

"For me, too," Andrew replies.

The dance finishes, and as they return to their table, a sophisticated sixty-five-year-old man approaches Isabella.

"I made it, finally," he says.

"What happened?"

"I took a few too many wrong turns," he replies.

"I'm glad you're here," she says, kissing him. "I want you to meet my husband, Andrew Wyler. Andrew, this is my uncle Robert Madison."

Evil Eyes

"It's a pleasure," Andrew says, shaking Robert's hand.

"Likewise," Robert replies. "Would you mind if I dance with my niece?"

"Please," Andrew says and kisses Isabella.

"I won't be gone long," Isabella says, and she and Robert start to dance.

"Are you happy for me, Uncle?"

"What are you doing, Isabella?"

"What do you mean? You know what I'm doing."

"Why can't you let this revenge thing go? You got what you wanted."

"Only part of what I wanted. But I'll have the rest soon."

"But why marry him?"

"You know getting married is every little girl's dream, Uncle. Besides, I need to keep him close until I'm done with him."

"None of this is going to bring your mother back."

"Or my stepsister either. We'll talk about this later. I've got to get back to my husband. And remember, if you know what's good for you, you won't say anything to Andrew," she says, walking off the dance floor and back to Andrew.

At the end of the reception, Andrew and Isabella walk around the ballroom, saying their goodbyes to the remaining guests, and the thirty-year-old catering manager approaches them with a bottle of champagne."

"Mr. And Mrs. Wyler, my name is Robin Samuels, and I'm the catering manager for the hotel. On behalf of the hotel, I want to congratulate you both on your marriage and give this bottle of champagne with our compliments."

"That's so nice of you and the hotel, Robin," Isabella says.

"Yeah, that's so nice," Andrew says, taking the bottle. "Now, all I need are a couple of glasses, and we're set for the honeymoon," he says, laughing."

"I need to use the bathroom before I drink anymore," Isabella says. "It was nice meeting you, Robin," she says and walks away.

As Isabella enters the bathroom and starts to fix her makeup in front of a mirror, Robin walks in and stands next to her.

"Your wedding was beautiful," Robin says.

"Thank you," Isabella replies.

"It reminded me of another wedding we catered in a town called Black Beach a few years ago."

When Isabella hears Black Beach, she pauses and looks at Robin in the mirror.

"Have you ever been to Black Beach? Mrs. Wyler," she asks.

Evil Eyes

"No, but it sounds like a special place," Isabella replies. "Andrew and I will have to go there sometime. If you'll excuse me, my husband's waiting for me," she says, puts her make-up away, and walks out of the bathroom.

Robin follows her back to the ballroom and approaches Isabella's uncle sitting alone at a table.

"Excuse me, aren't you Isabella's uncle?"

"That's right; I'm Robert Madison," he says, shaking her hand.

"It's nice meeting you, Mr. Madison. I'm Robin Samuels. I'm with the hotel," she says.

"Nice meeting you, Robin."

"Would you mind if I asked you a question?"

"Certainly."

"Did you ever live in a town called Black Beach?"

"I still do, for the past twenty-five years. I'm a pharmacist and have a pharmacy there. Do you know Black Beach?"

"Yes. My family lived there for a year when I was a sophomore in high school. What about your niece? Did she ever live there?"

"She did until she graduated from high school. You must have been there at the same time."

"Yeah, I must have," Robin says, looking at Isabella suspiciously.

"You should talk to her about it. I'm sure she'd love to reminisce."

"I'll do that. "Thank you," she says and walks away.

At the end of the night, Andrew, Isabella, and a few remaining guests are dancing as the song finishes and the bandleader speaks.

"Well, folks, that was our last song; on behalf of the band, we want to congratulate the bride and groom and wish them much happiness. Thank you."

"I'm going to change clothes for the honeymoon," Isabella says. "I'll be right back," she kisses him, picks up a small suitcase she has stored under the bandstand, and walks back into the bathroom.

As she starts changing her clothes, Robin walks into the bathroom.

"Getting ready for your honeymoon, Mrs. Wyler?"

"That's right," Isabella says with an annoyed tone.

"Going someplace romantic?"

"Not that's any of your business, but we're going to Europe," Isabella replies, looking at Robin's image in the mirror.

"That sounds so romantic. Well, I'll let you finish dressing," she says as she starts to leave the bathroom and then stops.

"Just one more thing," Robin says. "You were wrong to say you'd never been to Black Beach, Isabella."

Evil Eyes

"Is that right?" Isabella says, staring evilly at Robin's mirror image. "How do you know that?"

"Your uncle told me you lived there all through high school."

Isabella's demeanor changes to concern. "I love my uncle, but he's got a terrible memory, so you can't go by him." Isabella replies.

"You were a senior when I was a sophomore, but your name was Susan then, but I never forgot your eyes," Robin says. "They radiated evil even then."

Isabella stops changing and turns toward Robin.

"You're wrong," Isabella says as she stares at Robin. "I don't remember you because I didn't go to high school there."

"Does that mean you don't remember Mary Fredricks?"

"If I've never been in Black Beach, how would I know someone named Mary Fredricks?"

"You should remember her; you murdered her," Robin says. "You pushed her down a flight of stairs because she was going to tell the whole town about all the evil things you did."

Isabella increases the intensity of her stare. "You're right, Robin. I did go to school in Black Beach, and I do remember you and Mary. But I remember that her fall was determined to be an accident," she says, moving closer to Robin.

"That's bullshit. You did something to make the school think it was an accident. You were evil then, and you're still evil. Does your husband know about your past, Susan?"

"He's not interested in my past, just the future," Isabella says, smiling.

"Maybe not, but I'll talk to him and find out for myself."

She starts to walk out of the bathroom, and Isabella grabs her arm and pulls her back in.

"You're wrong about me murdering Mary because she's not dead," Isabella says.

"What are you talking about? I saw her buried."

"Then they didn't do a very good job. Look behind you."

Robin turned around, and Isabella made her see a young woman standing in the doorway. Shocked, Robin calls out to her.

"Mary, it can't be you," she says in disbelief. "You're dead."

As Robin walks toward the woman, the woman walks out of the bathroom, and Robin follows her. Watching and continuing her stare, Isabella follows Robin outside the hotel and watches the woman walk out onto a busy street.

Evil Eyes

"Mary, get out of the road," Robin says as she sees a car speeding down the road heading for the woman, and she runs out in the road to keep her from being hit and gets hit herself.

Isabella sees Robin's lifeless body in the middle of the road and smiles. "Say hi to Mary for me," she says as she walks back into the hotel.

Chapter Three

A couple of weeks later, Isabella, Andrew, and Night are driving down the main street of Black Beach. The town is a small, perfectly maintained, quaint-looking place near the ocean.

"So, this is Black Beach," Andrew says. "I never thought places like this existed."

"Beautiful, isn't it?" Isabella says.

"A picture," Andrew says. "But why such a morose name for such a pretty place?"

"Because at night, the ocean looks black. Park wherever you find a spot; my uncle's pharmacy is just up the street."

Andrew parks the car, and Isabella takes a tube of lipstick and a small mirror out of her purse.

"You take Night and go on ahead. I'll be a minute."

They share a kiss, and Andrew gets out of the car.

"Come on, boy," Andrew says to Night, and the dog jumps out of the car and follows Andrew up the street toward the pharmacy.

Evil Eyes

A sixty-five-year-old vagrant man, walking with a limp and his body and face disfigured with significant burn scars and wearing tattered clothes, walks up to Andrew and hands him a card. As Andrew looks at the card, Night starts to growl and bark at the man.

"Night, stop it," he says while he reads the card. "I'm homeless, deaf, and can't earn a living. Can you spare some change?"

Andrew smiles, reaches into his pocket, and takes out some money. Suddenly, the vagrant stares at Andrew as if he knows him and starts getting agitated.

"Here you go, old timer," Andrew says, handing the man a five-dollar bill.

The vagrant ignores the money and gets more agitated, trying to communicate with Andrew. Night begins to bark and snap at the vagrant, and Andrew pulls him away.

"Stop it," Andrew says sternly.

At that moment, Isabella walks up behind Andrew, facing the vagrant, and gives him a hateful look. Terrified, the vagrant quickly leaves.

"That was weird, Andrew says.

"What was?" Isabella asks.

"That vagrant acted as if he knew me."

"Well, you are pretty famous," Isabella says, grabbing his arm. "Let's go."

As they walk up to the pharmacy, Isabella looks at Night. "You stay outside and be a good boy. We'll be right back."

Night sits outside the pharmacy door while Isabella and Andrew walk inside. They see Robert, dressed in a lab coat, finishing with a customer and walking over.

"How was Europe?" he asks Isabella.

"It was amazing," she replies. "I couldn't have asked for a better honeymoon. Right, darling?"

"I was just sad we had to leave," Andrew says, kissing her.

"And now we're going to move into my beach house and work on having a baby," Isabella says.

"A Baby?" Robert says. "So soon?"

"No time like the present," she replies, smiling.

"How do you like our little town, Andrew?"

"It's a special place," Andrew says. "Not like the crowded, dirty city I grew up in."

"Yes, when Isabella was living here, she …"

"Andrew doesn't want to hear about that," Isabella says, cutting him off. "He needs to buy some film for his camera."

"Certainly," Robert says. "Let me show you."

Outside on the street, the vagrant, still agitated, is watching the pharmacy and writing something on a small paper pad. Inside the pharmacy, Isabella senses something, walks to a street-side window, looks out, and sees the vagrant. She gives him a stare, and he imagines his body is shaking uncontrollably, and his face is breaking out with large, festering sores. He drops the pad and limps away as Isabella goes back to Andrew.

"Did you find your film?"

"No, it's not out here," Robert says. "But I think I have it in the stockroom. I'll go find it."

"I'll come with you, Uncle," Isabella says. I need something for a headache. We'll be right back, sweetheart," Isabella says and follows Robert into the pharmacy stockroom.

The stockroom is populated with shelving and stocked with pills and pharmacy supplies. As they walk in, Isabella suddenly grabs her head in pain and has to sit down.

"I need some more pills," she says, grimacing.

"I just gave you a bottle a couple of weeks ago, and it was supposed to last a month," Robert says.

"I had to start taking two pills a day. One pill wasn't working anymore."

"That's because you're exerting yourself too much, and your seizures are getting more frequent."

"My exertion level is none of your fucking business. Just give me the pills."

Robert walks to one of the shelves, picks up a large bottle of pills, puts thirty in a small pill bottle, hands them to Isabella, and she takes two.

"That's the last supply I'll have for a while, so take them sparingly."

As the pill starts to work, Isabella takes a deep breath and regains her composure.

"Thank you, Uncle. I have to get back to Andrew."

"Before you go, I have something to show you," he says and picks up a newspaper with a headline reading 'Woman killed during famous photographers' wedding' and hands it to Isabella.

"What's this?"

"Look at it."

She reads the headline, "So?"

"The woman was Robin Samuels, the catering manager at your wedding."

"Like I said, so?" Isabella says coldly.

"She was hit by a car on the road next to the hotel, and you had something to do with it, didn't you?"

"She had to die. She recognized me from high school and was going to tell Andrew about my past."

"You didn't have to kill her. He wouldn't have believed her."

"Well, now there's no chance of that," she says, smiling. "Now, let's go back to Andrew. We've got to go."

They walk out of the stockroom and over to Andrew, holding a few rolls of film.

"I'm sorry, Andrew, I didn't have the film you wanted," Robert says. "I thought I did."

"No worries," Andrew replies. "These will do just fine. How much do I owe you?"

"Nothing," Robert replies. "Consider them another wedding gift."

"Thank you," he says and looks at Isabella. "Are you okay?"

"I'm fine; Uncle always knows how to make me feel better. Let's go. Bye, Uncle, "She says, kissing Robert on the cheek.

"We'll see you later," Andrews says. "And thanks again for the film.

As Isabella and Andrew leave the pharmacy, Robert walks to a street-side window, looks out, and watches them walk, hand in hand, down the street to their car. Then he looks across the street and sees the vagrant staring at him desperately.

The following week, Isabella, Andrew, Terry and his date, Abigail, are sitting are at the beach house having dinner on the patio beside the pool.

"Your house is so beautiful," Abigail says.

"Thank you. We like it, don't we, sweetheart?" Isabella says to Andrew.

"Love it," Andrew replies.

"Yeah, this is a special place, but aren't you two getting tired of honeymooning?" Terry asks. "It's been a couple of months."

"Sounds like you're jealous," Isabella says.

"Or envious," Andrew says, smiling.

"I can fix that," Abigail says and kisses Terry.

"That's what I'm afraid of," Terry replies.

"Come on, Abigail, help me clear the table and bring in the dessert," Isabella says as she and Abigail pick up the dinner dishes and enter the kitchen.

"How long have you and Abigail been seeing each other?" Andrew asks.

"A month," Terry replies.

"A whole month. Sounds serious. Is she a model?"

"No, she's a nurse. We met at my last physical and hit it off. She was impressed by my test results," Terry jokes. "Speaking of serious, it looks like marriage agrees with you."

"Yeah, it's great."

"I'm happy to hear that, but by now, you must need a dick transplant."

"I am getting a little antsy about getting back to work."

"Just say the word, and I'll get the camera rolling. Moretti is rolling out his new fall line next month, and he asked if you would shoot it."

Isabella and Abigail returned carrying a pie and coffee, set them on the table, and sat down.

"Shoot, what?" Isabella asks.

"Terry's tempting me to take an assignment," Andrew replies.

"That's right. We've got to get this couch potato peeled and back behind the camera. That goes for you, too, Isabella. I've got plenty of work."

"No, my modeling days are over. All I want to be now is a housewife and mother."

"Mother? Are you guys keeping something from us?" Terry asks.

"Not yet, but we're trying," Andrew replies.

"That's all the more reason to get you back to the ranks of the employed; supporting a family is expensive," Terry says.

"You're right. Set up the shoot."

"But sweetheart, we were planning on remodeling one of the guest rooms for the baby," Isabella says.

"I know, but I can do both."

"But there's always time to work later," Isabella says, getting annoyed.

"But I'm ready to go back to work now," Andrew replies, looking at Isabella.

"But you promised."

"We'll talk about it later," Andrew replied.

"I want to talk about it now," Isabella insists.

"I said later," Andrew says, giving her an irritated look.

"Yeah, you two talk about it and let me know," Terry says. "We should go, Abigail; it's late."

"Ready when you are," Abigail replies.

"You have to leave already?" Isabella says. 'You haven't had dessert."

No dessert for me. I've got a figure to watch," Terry says as he and Abigail prepare to leave.

"Are you kidding?" Andrew asks. "You're watching your figure?"

"Not mine, Abigal's," Terry replies, laughing. "Thanks for dinner, it was great. We'll get together again real soon." He says, kissing Isabella on the cheek and shaking Andrew's hand.

"It was so nice meeting the two of you," Abigail says.

"You, too," Isabella replies.

Evil Eyes

"I'll walk you out," Andrew says, escorting Terry and Abigail to the door.

"Thanks for coming," Andrew says.

"Thanks for having us," Terry replies.

"Yes, thank you," Abigail says.

"Watch this guy, Abigail; you need to keep in line," Andrew jokes.

"I'm not worried; I've got access to medication," Abigail replies, laughing.

"And that's the other reason I like her," Terry says, and they all laugh.

"And, Terry, set up that shoot."

"But Isabella said…" Terry replies.

"I said, set it up."

"You got it. I'll call you to confirm the specifics," Terry says, and he and Abigail leave.

Andrew walks back into the kitchen as Isabella is washing dishes.

"What's going on?" he asks.

"What do you mean?"

"Why'd you make a scene about me returning to work."

Isabella stops washing the dishes and looks at Andrew, visibly upset.

"I didn't make a scene. I expect you to keep your word when we decide on something. We agreed you'd wait to go back to work, and now you're going back on your word without discussing it with me. And you know how important having a baby is to me."

Seeing how upset Isabella is, Andrew hugs her. "You're right, I'm sorry. We made a plan, and I should have talked to you before I changed it. I'm sorry. Forgive me?"

"Of course," Isabella says, regaining her composure and kissing him. "And if you want to return to work, it's okay with me."

"Are you sure?"

"I'm sure."

"I'll tell you what, the shoot should only take a couple of days, and as soon as it's over, we'll stay focused on babymaking."

"And I'm going to hold you to it," Isabella says seriously.

"You won't have to," Andrew replies, kissing her.

Instead of the shoot lasting a couple of days, as Andrew said, on the day he was supposed to be home, the shoot wasn't finished and would take another couple of days. That night, Andrew and Terry are having a drink in the hotel bar.

"Is it just me, or are all European designers assholes?" Andrew asks.

"Yeah, I think it's in their DNA," Terry replies. "Have you told Isabella the shoot won't be done tomorrow like you promised?"

"I'm going to tell her tonight when I call her."

"Are you going to wear a bulletproof vest over your ears when she finds out?"

"She'll be fine," Andrew says and finishes his drink. "I'll see you in the morning."

Andrew returns to his room and calls Isabella, who is reading and petting Night.

"Hello."

"Hi, sweetheart," Andrew says.

"Hi, I was hoping it was you," Isabella replies. "I miss you."

"I miss you, too."

"I've got a special dinner planned for tomorrow when you get home."

"I won't be home tomorrow; the shoot won't be done; the designer is being an asshole."

"What do you mean?" Isabella says, getting upset. "You promised you'd be home."

"We need another couple of days."

"A couple more days?" Isabella asks, getting angry.

"I'm sorry. I'm not any happier than you are, but what can I do? I made a commitment."

"And you made a commitment to me, too. I knew this would happen."

"What would happen?"

"You'd start making excuses not to come home when you promised."

"That's crazy. I'm not making excuses. I took the job, and I've got to finish it. Don't be unreasonable."

"So, wanting you home and holding you to your promise is being unreasonable? I understand. Listen, I've got to walk Night, so I'll talk to you tomorrow," she said, hung up the phone, and looked at Night.

"Don't worry, Night, Daddy will be home sooner than he thinks," she says and smiles.

The following day, the shoot is in progress, and several models are dressed in designer clothes and posing while Andrew takes pictures. Sitting in the back of the room watching are Terry and Antonio Moretti, the fifty-year-old Italian designer and his beautiful young girlfriend. As Andrew takes pictures, the studio's back door opens, and Isabella walks in unnoticed and hides behind a clothes rack.

"Okay, now take off your jacket," Andrew says to one of the models.

The model removes her evening jacket and reveals a very sexy evening dress.

Evil Eyes

"That's it. Now give me a sexy pose," Andrew says, taking pictures while the model poses.

Isabella gives Andrew a stare, and he suddenly gets intense pains in his stomach.

"Shit!" he says and grabs his stomach.

Terry and Moretti come to check on him.

"What's wrong?" Terry asks.

"I don't know. I've got a sharp pain in my stomach."

Isabella stops her stare, and Andrew's stomach pain disappears.

"Do you need a doctor?" Moretti asks.

"No, the pains are gone. It must have been indigestion," Andrew replies.

"Too much pasta for lunch," Terry says jokingly.

"Can we finish the shoot, please," Moretti says.

"Absolutely," Andrew says as Moretti and Terry walk back to their seats, and Andrew starts taking pictures.

Isabella looks at Andrew again, and the pain comes back so strong that he doubles over and drops to his knees. The exertion causes Isabella to have a seizure, and she grabs her head in pain and holds onto the clothing rack to keep from falling. She takes her pills from her purse, takes three, the seizure stops, and she walks to Andrew, now lying on the floor with his eyes closed.

"What's the matter, sweetheart?" Isabella says, kneeling beside him.

Andrew opens his eyes and sees Isabella, Terry, and Moretti.

"Isabella, I'm so glad to see you. I keep getting these terrible stomach pains. They're gone now, but I think I need to see a doctor."

"Don't worry, I'll take care of you," she said, kissing him and giving him a sweet smile.

Later that day, Isabella and Andrew are waiting in a doctor's office waiting room.

"Are you okay?" Isabella asks Andrew.

"That barium tastes like shit," Andrew replies. "Where did you find this doctor?"

"My uncle referred him. He's supposed to be one of the best internists in the state."

"Thank you for helping me," Andrew says, grabbing her hand.

"For better or worse, remember," Isabella says, smiling.

"And I want to get back to better," Andrew says, kissing her.

A nurse comes into the waiting room and approaches Andrew and Isabella.

"Doctor, Maxey will see you know."

Evil Eyes

She escorts them into an inner office, and Steven Maxey, a sixty-year-old doctor, meets them.

"Well, doctor, did you see anything in the X-ray of my stomach?" Andrew asks.

"Yes. Let me show you," he puts an X-ray on a lighting board, and he and they look at it.

As they do, Isabella stares at the doctor and causes him to imagine he sees an ulcer in the X-ray that isn't there. "This spot is an ulcer," he says, pointing at the X-ray.

"And ulcer? Really?" Andrew asks.

"And it's a bad one," the doctor replies.

"But I've never had any problems with my stomach before. No acid indigestion or anything." Andrew says.

"That's peculiar, considering how advanced it is."

"What do you think caused it, Doctor," Isabella asks.

"Ulcers are caused by a virus that affects the stomach lining. And unless they're treated, the stomach lining gets infected, which causes the pain."

"What about stress?" Isabella asks. "Does that make them worse?"

"Yes. During treatment, you have to eliminate as much stress as possible. I'll prescribe something that will heal your stomach lining, but while it heals, you need to rest," the doctor says as he writes a prescription and gives it to Andrew.

"How long will it take to heal?"

"You should be back to normal in a month if you rest," the doctor replies.

"Oh, he'll rest," Isabella says. "I'll see to that."

Chapter Four

A few days later, Andrew was at home resting and having a cup of coffee on the poolside patio when he heard a knock at the front door. He opens the door and sees Robert.

"Good morning, Robert."

"Good morning. Can I come in for a minute?"

"Sure," he replies, and Robert walks into the house. "Isabella's not here; she's walking Night," Andrew says.

"I know. I spoke with her a few minutes ago. I came to see you."

"About what?"

"Can we sit down?" Roberts asks.

"Sure. Let's go out on the patio. Can I get you a cup of coffee? I'm having one."

"No, thank you. I've already had plenty."

"Follow me," Andrew says, leading Robert out to the patio, where they sit.

"Peaceful, huh?" Andrew asks.

"Very. Isabella told me about your ulcer. How are you feeling?"

"Better since I've started taking medication and getting some rest."

"That's good. Listen, Andrew, I've wanted to talk to you for a while, and I know that what I'm going to tell you will be hard to comprehend, but there are things about Isabella you need to know."

"What things?"

"For starters, her real name isn't Isabella; it's Susan."

"What? Why does she call herself Isabella?"

"To cover up her past."

"Why would she need to cover up her past?"

"Because before she met you, she was institutionalized for ten years, and she doesn't want you to know."

"Institutionalized? Is this a joke?"

"Trust me; it's no joke. Isabella, I mean Susan, experienced severe brain trauma in the car accident that killed her mother, and she suffers from brain seizures. She was institutionalized while she underwent treatments."

"What kind of seizures?" Andrew questions.

"They're brought on by severe exertion, and when they happen, the pain in her head can be so strong sometimes she loses consciousness and falls."

"And that's what causes the headaches."

"That's right. She takes seizure medication to control them, but it's not working."

"But why not tell me about all this herself?"

"There's more. Besides her mother being a model, she practiced witchcraft and taught Susan to do it as well. So, while in the institution, she focused on her witchcraft and developed powers."

"Witchcraft and powers? What do you mean?"

"She can manipulate people's minds."

"In what way?" Andrew asked.

"She can make people do and see things that aren't there. Like your ulcer."

"My ulcer was real. I saw it."

"You and the doctor saw what Isabella wanted you to see. Have you ever had stomach problems before?"

"No, I only started having problems on this shoot I was on. But why make me think I had an ulcer?"

"It's part of her plan to control and keep you trapped while she gets her revenge."

"Revenge? For what?"

"For what your father did. Susan's mother was married to my brother, and after he died of cancer, she became a model to support herself and met your father on a photo shoot in Los Angeles thirty years ago, and they had an affair when Susan was thirteen."

"My father had an affair with Susan's mother and got her pregnant? I don't believe it. My dad wouldn't cheat on my mother."

"I told you this would be hard to accept, but it's all true. During the affair, my sister-in-law got pregnant with your father's baby, and he promised to divorce your mother so they could be together. But he lied to her and went back to his wife and left her alone to have the baby. That's when the accident happened that killed both Susan's mother and the unborn baby and almost killed Susan."

"You expect me to believe all this bullshit?" Andrew says.

"Ask your father," Robert says.

"My dad's dead," Andrew replies.

"No, he's not. Remember that old vagrant you met in Black Beach?"

"The deaf guy?"

"That's right. He's your father, or what's left of him."

"That's not possible. My dad and mom were burned alive in a car accident."

"Did they ever find their bodies?"

"No, they were incinerated when the car blew up."

"Burnt beyond recognition, just like the man you met."

Evil Eyes

"But what did Susan have to do with it?"

At that moment, Isabella walks onto the patio with Night.

"Go ahead, Uncle, don't stop now; tell him everything," she said.

"No, you tell me," Andrew says to Susan.

"Let's just say I'm finally getting my revenge. Your father screwed my mother, got her pregnant, then dumped her and left her to take care of herself, which is what caused the accident we had. Yes, somehow, I survived the accident, but the damage to my head caused me to have debilitating seizures. I was put in an institution, and for the next ten years, I underwent shock therapy to get them to stop, and I almost went crazy. But it is true when they say whatever doesn't kill makes you stronger because I turned my suffering into strength beyond comprehension, isn't that right, Uncle?"

Robert turns away and doesn't answer.

"And every second of every day in that institution, all I ever thought about was getting out and finding your father and getting even with him for what he did to my mother, my unborn stepsister, and me."

"Did you cause the accident my parents were in?" Andrew asks.

"I can't take all the credit. Your father was drunk and hit a tree. But unfortunately for him, he lived, and I found him. And now that I have you, we'll have a little family reunion."

"You bitch. I'll kill you," Andrew screamed and ran toward her.

She gives him a stare, and he collapses.

"That's good. You want to hurt me, but it's hard to do without legs."

Andrew looks down at his legs and watches his pants disappear, and his legs start to disintegrate. Screaming in pain, he sees his skin fall off, and his bones break and then run to dust.

"Fight it, Andrew. It's not real; it's just your imagination," Robert says.

"I can't," Andrew screams.

"Of course, you can't," she says. "And neither can you, uncle, remember. Now get the fuck out of here before I forget you're my uncle and do something to you, you'll regret."

"But you can't …"

"I said go," she says and gives him a look.

"I'm sorry, Andrew," he says and leaves.

Andrew continues to scream as she walks over to him.

"And as easily as I made it happen, I can make it stop. Look at your legs now."

The pain stops, and he watches his legs and pants return. At that moment, Isabella starts to have a seizure, grabs her head in pain, slumps to the floor, and crawls to her purse. She takes out her pills and takes four pills before her seizure stops. Andrew regains reality and stands.

"Look, I didn't know anything about my dad having an affair. I wasn't around."

"Doesn't matter. He took away my family, and I swore to take his. And now that I have you, that's what I'm doing."

"Wait a minute, did you kill Elizabeth to get her out of the way so you could get to me."

"That's right. I didn't have a choice. She wasn't going to give you up."

"And you made Maria think she was on fire so you could take her place on the shoot."

"No, I made her think she was on fire because she pissed me off. And to take her place," she says, smiling.

"And the caterer, why her?"

"She knew too much about me that I didn't want to share."

"You're insane."

"And as soon as I get pregnant, you and your daddy will die, too."

"I won't have a baby with a psychopath like you."

"I might be a psychopath, but your father made me that way. And the name is Isabella, not Susan."

"You can't keep me here," he says desperately.

"Do you want more proof that I can?"

Realizing she's right, Andrew doesn't say anything.

"I didn't think so. Now I need to go to the market in Black Beach, and you're going with me," she says, and they leave the house.

Andrew, Isabella, and Night arrive at Black Beach and park in front of a market near Robert's pharmacy.

"Do you need anything from the market?" Isabella asks Andrew.

"If they sell guns, pick one up for me," he says sarcastically.

Isabella ignores his comment and gets out of the car.

"I'll be right back, so don't try anything stupid, like trying to get help. If you do, what happened to your legs before will happen to your whole body over and over again," she says and gets out of the car.

"Let's go, Night," she says, and Night jumps out of the car and follows her into the market.

When they are out of sight, Robert walks up to the car.

"Andrew, I want to show you something. Come with me."

Evil Eyes

"Fuck you. I don't trust you. You didn't tell me about Susan until it was too late."

"Believe me, I told you as soon as I could. I didn't know what she planned until you two were married. Now, please come with me; it's important. Hurry before she finishes at the market.

Andrew exits the car and follows Robert into the pharmacy through a back door.

"Go into the stockroom. I'll keep a look out for Susan."

Andrew walks into the stockroom, and the vagrant comes out from behind a shelving unit with a note in his hand. He hands it to Andrew.

The note says, "I'm your father, Nathan Wyler. And I'm so sorry for what I did."

Andrew tears up the note.

"So, you did have an affair with Susan's mother and got her pregnant?"

Nathan pauses and then nods his head yes.

"You know you caused my mother's death, and for what? A piece of ass," Andrew says angrily.

Richard takes another piece of paper out and hands it to Andrew.

"I'm not proud of what I did, and the guilt I've had to live with has caused me more pain than anything

Susan has done to me. Please forgive me," he says with tears running down his face.

Andrew sees the suffering his father's been through, and tears form in his eyes.

"Dad, I love you."

The two men hug as Robert's voice is heard.

"Andrew, you have to leave."

Andrew and Nathan walk out of the stockroom.

"I want you to have this," he says, handing Andrew a small plastic bag of white powder.

"What is this?"

"It's a sedative. Put it in her coffee, and it will knock Susan out long enough for you to escape."

"Are you sure it's strong enough? You know how powerful she is."

"If she drinks all of this, she'll be unconscious for a couple of hours. Make sure not to let Night see you give it to her. He'll try and stop you from leaving."

"Thank you for helping me, Robert. I know you're taking a risk."

"I'm just sorry I didn't do it sooner. Now, you need to get back to the car."

Andrew looks at his father. "When I leave, I'm taking you with me."

Evil Eyes

They hug one another, and Andrew goes out the back door and back to the car.

The following day, Andrew sits on the patio looking at the bag of powder. As Night comes out to the patio, he puts it in his shirt pocket.

"Well, good morning, old buddy," Andrew says, petting Night as his cell phone rings, and he answers it.

"Hello, Terry. Thanks for calling me back. Just give me a minute," he says, walking back into the house, away from Night.

"I need you to pick me up, but I'll have to call you back and tell you when. Okay, thanks," he says, hanging up as Isabella walks in.

"Who were you talking to," she asks.

"Terry, he was asking me to play racquetball."

"What did you say?"

"I said I couldn't play and needed to rest."

"That's good. You don't want to get him involved, for his sake."

"Listen, I made some coffee, so let's sit on the patio and enjoy it and then get back to babymaking," he says, forcing a smile.

"I'm so glad to hear you say that," she replies.

"I know I can't do anything, so I might as well give in," he says.

"That's right, and you might even enjoy it," she replies, smiling.

"Go out on the patio, and I'll bring out the coffee," he says, "Night's already out there."

Susan walks out to the patio, and Andrew pours two cups of coffee, puts the sedative into one of the cups, then brings them out to the patio, and hands the sedative-laced coffee to Susan.

"Thank you," she says.

"You're welcome," he says and sits beside her.

"It's a beautiful morning, isn't it?" She says as she drinks the coffee.

A couple of minutes later, Susan starts to feel the effects of the sedative and becomes dizzy and shuts her eyes.

"I feel strange," she says, looking at her coffee cup, "Did you?"

Before she could finish her statement, she passed out, and Andrew quickly walked back into the house, locked the patio door, leaving Night outside with Susan, and then called Terry.

"Terry, you have to come to the beach house and pick me up; Isabella's trying to kill me."

Chapter Five

Terry arrives at the house, and Andrew walks out carrying a duffel bag and gets in the car.

"Man, what happened to you? You look like shit," Terry says.

"I'll tell you about it later, but we have to go now."

"Where," Terry asks as they drive down a narrow road next to a cliff.

"To Black Beach to pick someone up," Andrew says.

"Black Beach? Where the hell is that?"

"I'll show you, just drive."

"And who are we picking up?"

"My father."

"Your father? Nathan Wyler? You know he's dead, right?"

"No, he's alive."

"Are you sure the problem in your stomach hasn't gone to your brain?"

"No, Isabella has powers and has kept him alive and deformed since his accident, and she's going to kill us both as soon as she gets pregnant.

"Man, you're terrified," Terry says.

"Yes, I am terrified because of what she can do."

"Okay, that's it, we're not going to any Black Beach. We're going to the hospital to get you checked out."

"Look, I know it sounds crazy; I thought so, too until she used her powers on me. You've got to trust me, my father, and I need to get away from her."

"I might not believe you, but I'll do whatever I can to make sure you and your father are safe from that bitch."

"Thank you, Terry. I'm sorry I had to drag you into this."

"You didn't drag me. And if you're sorry, you can thank me with a bottle of scotch later," Terry says, smiling.

At that moment, Terry starts to cough uncontrollably and has a hard time breathing.

"Are you okay?" Andrew asks.

"Yeah, my throat is just dry," Terry replies, continuing to cough as he looks in the rearview mirror and sees his face break into large, painful blisters. "What the fuck?" he says and screams out in pain.

"What's the matter?" Andrew asks.

"Would do you mean? Can't you see the sores on my face?"

Not seeing anything wrong with Terry's face, Andrew realizes the sores are in his imagination.

"It's Isabella," Andrew says. "She must have woken up and is making you see the sores. They're not real. They're in your imagination."

Terry sees his face completely covered with sores.

"Imagination, my ass. They're real," he screams as he concentrates on his face and inadvertently steps on the gas pedal, and the car speeds down the road.

"Slow down," Andrew yells, seeing that Terry is losing control of the car.

Terry continues to scream as he imagines the skin on his head starting to peel off. He lets go of the steering wheel and the car speeds toward the cliff.

"Terry, watch out," Andrew yells. He grabs the steering wheel to steer the car away from the cliff, but before he can, the car falls over the cliff, lands on the ground below, and explodes.

Andrew is sitting on the patio alone, sleeping. He wakes up, hoping the car accident was just a dream, and calls Terry's office.

"Hello, Cindy, it's Andrew. Yeah, I feel better. Is Terry there? What? When?" As he listens, he becomes angry, hangs up the call, and screams.

"No," he yells, walks back into the kitchen, and grabs a butcher knife.

Susan is in bed with Night when Andrew knocks on the door.

"Come in," she says.

Andrew walks into the bedroom, hiding the knife behind his back, and walks over to the bed.

"What's the matter," she asks, seeing Andrew's anger.

"You fucking, bitch, you murdered Terry."

"You're to blame for that. I warned you not to get him involved."

"I'm going to kill you," Andrew says as he shows the knife and goes to the bed to stab her.

She gives him a look, and he freezes.

"You shouldn't play with knives; you can hurt yourself."

She looks at him again and Andrew stops, turns the knife around and stabs himself in the shoulder.

"Fuck," he screams out in pain, drops the knife, and falls to the floor.

"You still don't get it. You can't get away from me, not until one of us is dead," she says with an evil laugh.

Evil Eyes

Later that day, Andrew is in bed, sleeping with his shoulder bandaged. Isabella walks into the room carrying a tray of food, and Andrew wakes up.

"What do you want?" he asks.

"You slept through lunch, so I brought you something to eat," she says, setting the tray on the nightstand.

Andrew sets up and grabs his shoulder in pain.

"Why is my shoulder bandaged? The wound is just in my imagination."

"Not anymore. My powers have gotten stronger, so now the torture and pain I cause won't be in your imagination. It will be real. Now eat your lunch. I'm meeting my uncle for coffee in Black Beach," she says, leaving the room.

As soon as she's gone, Andrew gets out of bed, puts on his clothes, goes on the balcony, and watches her drive away with Night. At that moment, Robert drives up to the house and Andrew goes downstairs to meet him.

"What are you doing here? I thought you were supposed to meet Susan in Black Beach?"

"I told her that to get her away from the house. What happened to your shoulder?" Roberts asked.

"Susan made me stab myself."

"You mean it wasn't in your imagination?"

"No. She's gotten more powerful and can make you do things that aren't in your imagination."

"Did you give her the sedative?"

"Yes, but it didn't last. She knew I tried to leave with Terry and murdered him."

"I know, she told me about it. I'm so sorry," Robert says as he shows his car keys to Andrew. "Your dad's waiting outside in my car. I want you to take my car and go somewhere she won't find you, and I'll take care of Susan when she returns."

"But she'll know you helped me again and do something terrible to you."

"I'll take my chances. She has to be stopped," he says, handing Andrew his car keys.

"Thank you," Andrew says. "And good luck," he says, leaving the house and getting in the car.

Andrew's father sits in the passenger seat, and Andrew hugs him.

"Don't worry, Dad, I'll take care of you," he says, starting the car.

As he starts to back out of the driveway, Susan pulls up behind him, stops him from leaving, and she and Night get out of the car.

"You and Daddy aren't going anywhere. Let's all go back into the house.

"No, Susan," Robert says, taking out a gun and pointing it at her. "I should have stopped you a long time

Evil Eyes

ago. I'm sorry you ended up the way you are, but your evil can't go on," he says.

"Go ahead, you old fool; I'm tired of your meddling."

Robert fires, and Andrew watches the bullet come out of the gun in slow motion, stop in mid-air, then turn back toward Robert and hit him in the chest, killing him.

"Once again, you're to blame for another death," she smiles. "Now, let the three of us go back into the house and have that family reunion."

Andrew, Nathan, Night, and Susan go back into the house.

"Now, let's get this party started," she says, looking at Richard, and he doubles over in pain and falls to the floor. "It hurts, doesn't it?"

"Stop it," Andrew screams as he goes to his dad.

"Since your father means so much to you, I think you should look more like him," she says, looking at Andrew.

Andrew's body becomes deformed like his father's, and he screams in pain. While Susan is distracted with Andrew, Nathan fights through his pain, stands up, grabs Susan by the throat, and chokes her. As Susan gasps for air, falls to the floor, and starts to have a seizure, Night jumps on Nathan's back and starts biting him. Letting go of Susan, Nathan fights with the dog, and they end up outside on the pool patio. As Night continues attacking Nathan viciously, he backs into the patio railing and falls over the steep embankment next to the pool with Night still on his back.

As Susan writhes in pain from the seizure, she struggles to get to her handbag for her pills. Andrew gets up, runs out to the patio, looks over the railing, and sees his father on the ground dead, but he doesn't see Night. He goes back into the house, picks up Robert's gun, walks over to Susan, grabs her purse, and takes out the pills.

"I've got good news for you; you won't need these anymore," he says, dumping the pills on the floor and stomping on them.

She looks up at him, and before she can stare at him, he shoots her. At that moment, Night walks into the room, and Andrew points the gun at him, expecting him to attack. Instead of attacking, Night whimpers, walks over, and licks Andrew's hand.

"So, she was controlling you, too, wasn't she?" he says, petting the dog."

A few weeks later, Andrew, his body back to normal, walks into a trendy restaurant and sits at the bar.

"How's it going, Mr. Wyler? I haven't seen you in a while. You been on vacation?"

"No, Jimmy, just tied up. I'll have my usual but make it a double."

"One double scotch and water coming up."

Evil Eyes

The bartender makes the drink and hands it to Andrew as a beautiful young blonde sits beside him. Andrew has his drink, not looking at the woman.

"Excuse me, I don't want to seem forward, but aren't you Andrew Wyler, the fashion photographer?"

Andrew doesn't look at her and continues drinking.

"Yes."

"My name is Andrea, and I'm a model."

"No kidding," he replies coldly.

"You probably don't remember, but I did a photo shoot with you a couple of years ago, and because of the shots you took, my career took off."

"I'm happy for you," he says, trying to ignore her, and looks at the bartender. "I'll have another one, Jimmy."

"Can I buy you a drink?" The woman says.

"No, thank you," he replies as the bartender makes the drink.

"Please, it's the least I can do for what you did for me."

"Okay," Andrew says.

"And what will have you?" The bartender asks the woman.

"I'll have a black Russian."

Hearing her drink order, Andrew looks at her and sees that she has deep, captivating black eyes. He freezes, terrified.

THE END

www.ingramcontent.com/pod-product-compliance
Lightning Source LLC
LaVergne TN
LVHW040158080526
838202LV00042B/3223